D0337229

ALLEY CATS
Cousin Archie
Uncle Bertie
Hattie
Auntie Lucy
Lenny & Lulu

Little Lost Lenny

Written by Lesley Rees
Illustrated by Terry Burton

Bright ☆ Sparks

One grey day, Lenny, the kitten, was happily chasing his twin sister, Lulu, around the higgledy-piggledy, messy alley. They were having great fun, leaping over boxes and jumping through tyres.

Hattie, their mummy, looked up at the big, dark clouds. "I think we had better tidy up before it rains," she said. "Come on, everyone, let's put everything away."

So Uncle Bertie and Cousin Archie moved the boxes.

Auntie Lucy helped Hattie tidy away the blankets. Even little Lulu helped by clearing away her toys – she didn't want the rain to make them squelchy and soggy!

Everyone was busy helping… or were they?

That little mischief-maker, Lenny, was planning something naughty! He hid behind Lulu's dustbin, then leapt out and grabbed her teddy.

With a giggle, he ran off down the alley. Lulu gave a long wail. Teddy was her favourite toy.

“Mummy!” she yelled. “Lenny’s got my teddy!”

Lenny stopped at the bottom of the alley and called to his sister.

"If you want Teddy," he said, "come and get him."

Lulu raced down the alley.

Lenny giggled and tossed the teddy high into the sky.

He went straight over his sister's head and disappeared behind a large fence!

Lulu stood and wailed until all the other cats came charging down the alley.

Lenny knew he was going to be in *big* trouble.

“Whatever’s the matter?” cried Hattie.
The little kitten sobbed and told her
mummy what her naughty brother had done.

Everyone looked at Lenny.

"Lenny, you really are a naughty pussy!" said his mother, crossly. "You know you're not supposed to come down to this part of the alley."

Bertie scooped up Lulu. “Don’t worry,” he said, kindly.
“Archie and I will find Teddy for you later.”

Lenny stood still, bit his lip and trembled.

“Why do you have to get into so much trouble?” asked Hattie. “And why can’t you be more helpful like your sister?” And off she stomped, back towards her dustbin.

“Sorry, Mummy,” whispered Lenny.

A big, fat tear trickled down his cheek.

"It's not fair," he thought. "I didn't mean to lose silly old Teddy!"

Lenny gave a sniff and wandered over to the gate. He peeped through the bars. Mummy had said that they must never, *ever* go through this gate.

“But I don’t know why,” thought Lenny.

"I do know that Teddy's in there, though," he said, "and I must try and get him back."

So he squeezed himself through the bars...

Lenny found himself standing at the edge of a big building site. There were wooden planks and piles of bricks everywhere – Lenny thought it looked great fun.

“I don’t know why Mummy told me to keep away from here,” he laughed. “It’s like having my very own adventure playground.”

The naughty pussy soon forgot about feeling sad as he climbed ladders and walked across gangplanks, high above the ground.

"I'm Lucky Lenny the Pirate!" he laughed. Then he stopped and peered through the rain.

"And there's Teddy!" he cried.

As Lenny grabbed the bear,
the plank tipped up.

The rain had made it very
slippery and…

down,

down,

down

he fell –
all the way
to the bottom
of a mucky,
muddy hole.

Luckily, cats always
land on their feet,
so he wasn't hurt,
but he'd had
a real fright!

Lenny's little claws tried to grip the sides of the hole, but the rain had loosened the soil. It sprinkled down all over his head!

Oh dear, now he really *was* stuck!

"Mummy! Mummy!" he meowed. "Help!"

Meanwhile, back in the alley, the cats were sheltering from the rain. Suddenly, Hattie looked round.

"Where's Lenny?" she asked the others. But no-one had seen him for ages.

Hattie ran out into the alley. "Lenny!" she cried through the pouring rain. "Lenny, where are you?"

She knew something was wrong.

“Go and get the dogs,” she said to Archie. “Ask them to help us find my poor, little Lenny.”

Archie quickly returned with Harvey and the gang.

"Don't worry, Hattie," said Harvey. "We'll soon find him for you."

All the dogs and cats ran out into the pouring rain, meowing and barking Lenny's name.

At the bottom of the alley, the Old English Sheepdog, Ruffles, sniffed.

"I can smell him!" he yelped. "He's very near!"

He snuffled to the gate. "Yes, he's in there!" cried Patchy, the dog with a patch over one eye, "I can hear him crying!"

The animals rushed through the gate and quickly found the muddy hole where Lenny was stuck.

"Don't worry!" called Harvey. "We'll soon get you out."

Uncle Bertie found a thick rope. "We can use this," he called.

Ruffles, Harvey and Bertie lowered the rope to Lenny. The tiny kitten clung on tight and was pulled to safety.

Lenny gave Teddy back to Lulu. "I didn't mean to make you sad," he said.

"We were *so* worried!" said Hattie. "No special kitty treats for you tonight."

"I'm really sorry, Mummy," sniffed Lenny.

Hattie smiled and gave her naughty, little kitten a big hug. "That's okay," she smiled. "At least you're safe now." Then, all the Alley Cats went back to the alley for lots of cat-napping!

The End

This is a Bright Sparks Book
First published in 2001
BRIGHT SPARKS, Queen Street House, 4 Queen Street, Bath BA1 1HE, UK

Copyright © PARRAGON 2001

Created and produced by THE COMPLETE WORKS,
St. Mary's Road, Royal Leamington Spa, Warwickshire CV31 1JP, UK

All rights reserved.
No part of this publication may be reproduced, stored in a retrieval system,
or transmitted by any means, electronic, mechanical, photocopying, recording or otherwise,
without the prior permission of the copyright holder.

Printed in China

ISBN 1-84250-195-X